The Snowman Storybook

With words by Raymond Briggs

Random House 🏠 New York

http://www.randomhouse.com/

Library of Congress Cataloging-in-Publication Data
Briggs, Raymond.
Snowman storybook / words and pictures by Raymond Briggs.
p. cm. — (A Random House pictureback)
ISBN 0-679-88343-6 (pbk.)
SUMMARY: When his snowman comes to life, a little boy invites him into his home and in return is taken on a flight high above the countryside. Unlike the original edition, this version has words.
[1. Snowmen—Fiction.] I. Title.
[PZ7.B7646Snp 1997] [E]—dc20 96-16076

Printed in the United States of America 10 9 8 7 6 5

In the morning James woke to see snow falling. He ran into the garden as fast as he could, and he started to make a snowman.

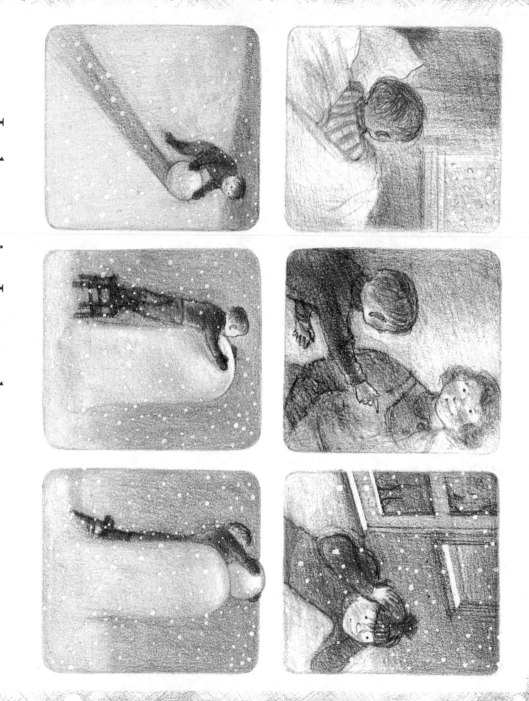

He gave him a scarf and a hat, a tangerine for a nose, and lumps of coal for his buttons and his eyes.

What a wonderful snowman he was! James could not go to sleep because he was thinking of his snowman.

In the middle of the night he crept down to see the snowman again. And suddenly . . . the snowman *moved*!

"Come in," said James. "But you must be very quiet."

The snowman was amazed by everything he saw.

They even went into James's mother and father's bedroom.

And the snowman dressed up in their clothes.

Suddenly, the snowman took James by the hand and ran out of the house, across the snow,

and up, up into the air.
They were flying!

James and the snowman flew for miles through the cold, moonlight air.

Then they landed gently on the snow, home safe in the garden.

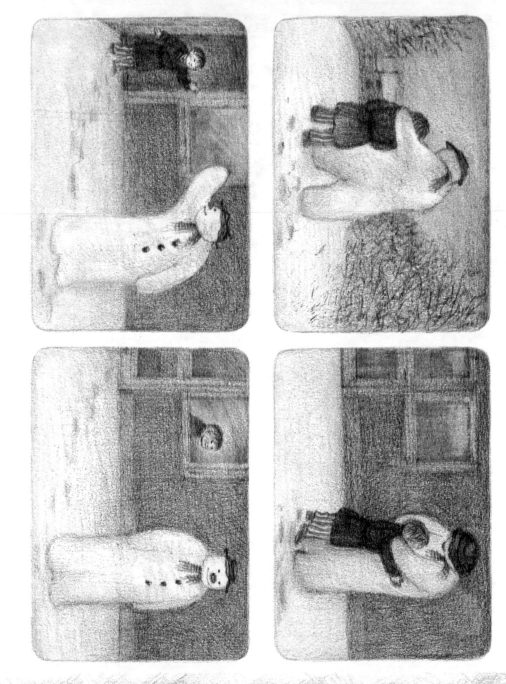

James gave the snowman a hug and said good night.

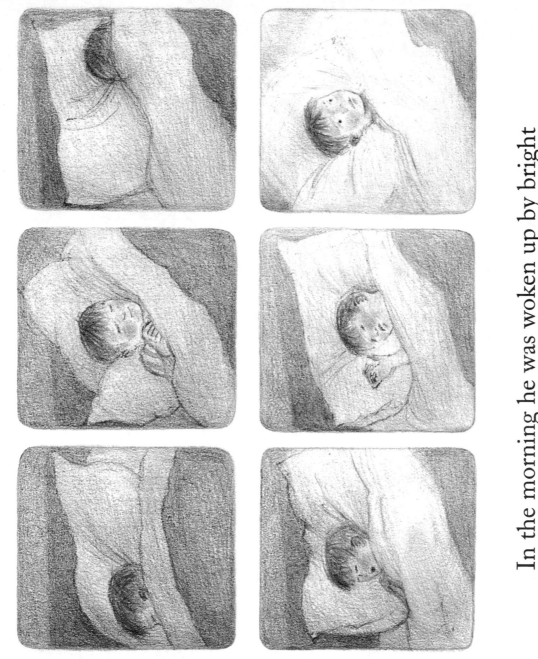

In the morning he was woken up by bright sunlight shining on his face.

He must see the snowman again! James ran out of his room, down the stairs,

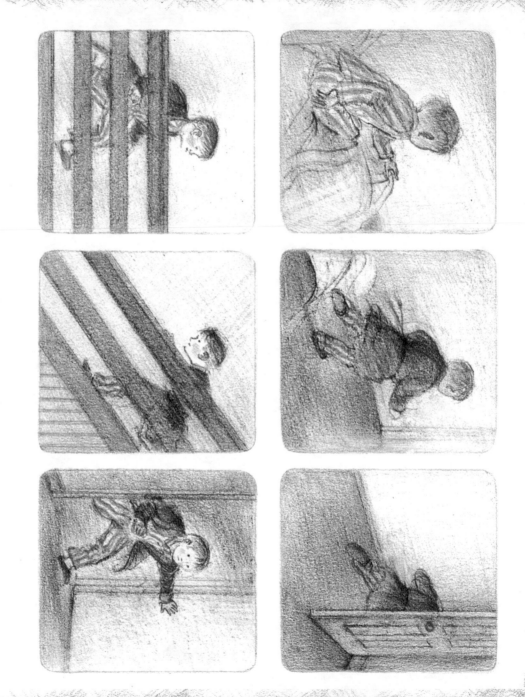

across the living room, past his mother
and father,

and into the garden.